CHICKYPOOH™

"Hi, I'm Chickypooh. I'm the chick with a leash on my kitty. Follow me, read my book series as I tour city to city."

"I want to teach you ways to protect yourself and to abstain. Abstain means to resist anything improper. Don't do it. Refrain!"

"There's an abundance of delightful anecdotes, illustrations, rhymes, and reasons to turn this page. No matter your race, creed, or if you're 9 to 99 in age."

"My advice is obvious; you'll see. By applying it, it will help to set you free."

ACKNOWLEDGEMENTS

We gratefully acknowledge all individuals and organizations who are working diligently to protect our children and to put a necessary end to bullying.

CHICKYPOOH ™

THE BULLY IN THE WHITE HOUSE

It's Worse Than You Think!

Jacqueline Charmane

GENRE: REALISTIC FICTION

This book is a work of realistic fiction. All information and opinions expressed herein are the views of the author. This publication is not intended to provide accurate and authoritative information concerning the subject matter covered and is for informational purposes only. Neither the author nor the publisher is attempting to provide legal advice of any kind.

DEDICATION

This book is dedicated to those who have experienced bullying; either as a bully or by being bullied. Bullying behavior is unacceptable. By exposing the behavior, we are sending a world-wide message that says, "we see you, we know you, and we want to help you."

FORWARD

For years, Evangelist Jacqueline Charmane has let her light so shine before men so that they may see her Good Works and Glorify God. By using her latest edition in the Chickypooh Series, to shine a light on an epidemic in the country, bullying, she has captured the essence and the importance of dealing with critical issues through the arts. The Bully In The White House is an outstanding book that can serve an excellent example of Celebrating African American History by honoring the accomplishments of President Barack Obama and First Lady Michelle Obama.

Evangelist Charmane skillfully juxtaposes the grace and dignity by which the First African American President served, against the present lack of respect shown for all Americans who have the utmost love for their Country.

The Bully In The White House presents a golden opportunity to educate the masses about the importance of loving thy neighbor as thyself, while always upholding the following truth 2 Timothy 1:7 "For God has not given us a spirit of fear but of power, love and a sound mind." As long as we live by these words, bullies all throughout the land will be defeated.

State Representative Sherry Dorsey Walker (Delaware House of Representatives - 3rd District)

Chickypooh visits The White House, in hopes she can get an answer to the Nation's question, "Why?" First, she must see how she can get into The White House, as a clever spy.

So, she disguises herself as The White House Shrink. What she discovers— you won't believe—it's worse than you think.

To make sure she's right, Chickypooh must cross the thin red line. What she's aiming to expose is not "fake news" or that which she heard from a "grapevine."

The hatred, bitterness, anger, and sickness that's in just one man's heart. It's like ten trillion sharp, poisonous, out-of-control darts.

Chickypooh decided to pretend to put her doctor's degree into use. In three sessions, she instructed each worker to lay down on the sofa, then hypnotized each one to get their minds loose.

She began by asking the first worker to think back 10 years ago to get a baseline to compare. Ten years ago, is when our Nation installed our first African American President, to take over the Oval Office chair.

Chickypooh started there, to see if she'd hear any negative feedback. But, on the contrary, they each wanted to award him a trophy and a plaque.

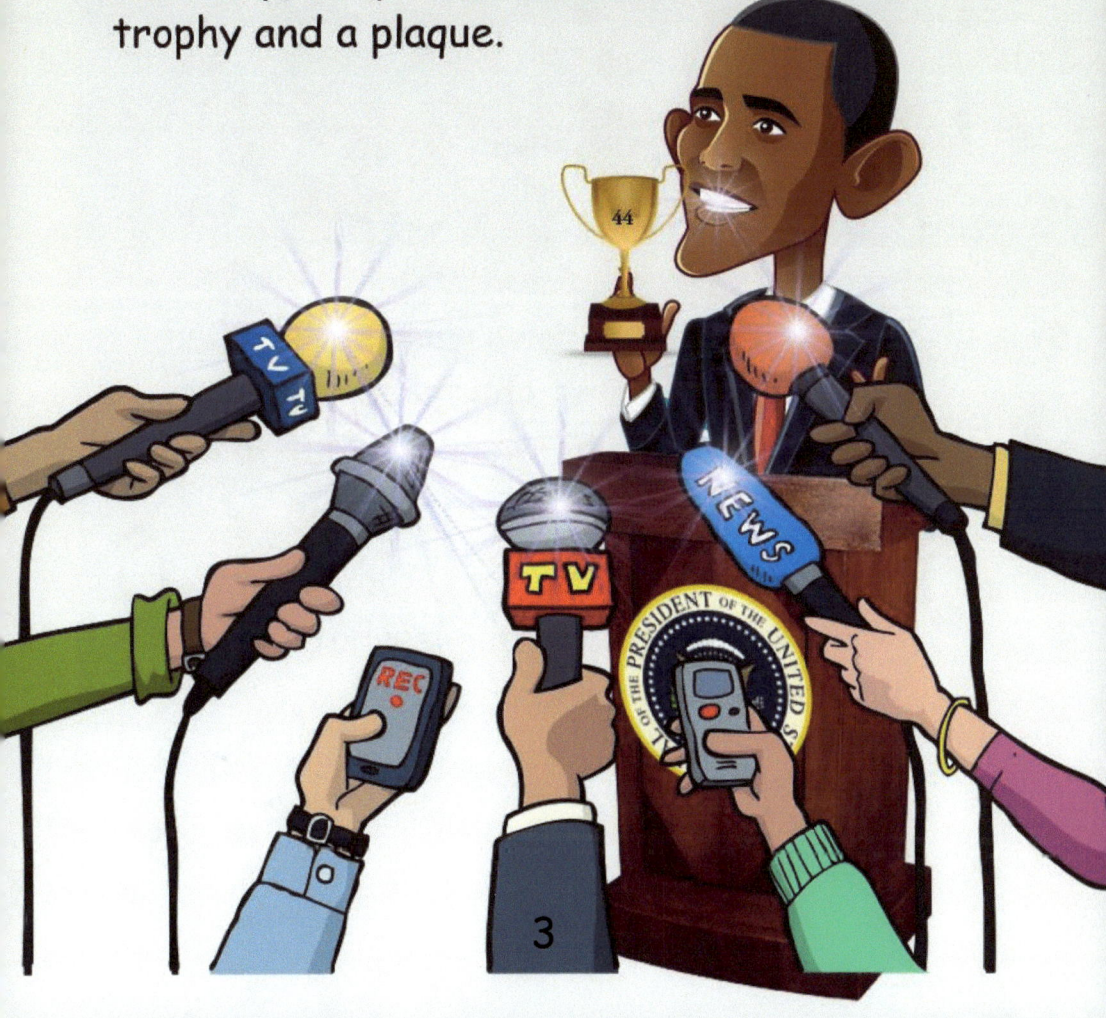

The first to lay down was the Butcher, who heard the most childhood tells. Initially, though, he was reluctant to come out of his secret shell.

Once he heard the soft, soothing, hypnotic music play. This is what the faithful Butcher had to say:

As a young boy, he was asked by his teacher, "What do you want to grow up to be?" He said very proudly, "The President of the United States would be the best job for me."

His teacher replied, "I'm afraid you have to choose another because the job as President is for white men. So, that will never happen for you since you don't have the right colored skin."

YES YOU CAN!

"What does that mean?" he said confused, as he looked straight into her eyes. "My momma said, 'I can be anything I want to be up until the day I die.'"

"When I die, what I've done will speak for my worth. From the ending to the middle, right from the beginning of my birth."

"So, I rather keep believing my momma who said 'Yes I Can!' I hope you don't punish me by putting me in the horrifying corner to stand."

"If you do, it's okay, because, in the dark, lonely corner, I'll see the obstacles that may come my way. In the corner, I'll do what my momma said, that is to close my eyes and pray."

"While In the corner, I'll have my back to the children who'll grow up learning to hate. However, they'll only see my back, which will block them from seeing the wonderful possibilities of my fate."

"What I'll see while I face the corner is what others deemed as the impossible dream. I won't be discouraged by the evil in their eyes or be distracted by their scheme."

His teacher stood, shocked by what she heard, she pulled out her biggest paddle. She lifted her hand and screamed, "How dare you sass me!" Then told him to face the wall and straddle.

"I'll straddle," he said, "but know the scars you leave will make me more determined to succeed. Every hurt, pain, disgrace and shame will give me more unbeatable courage to lead."

Thirty-five years later came a day most people thought they would never see. Yes, it was him, an African American man sitting in the White House sipping tea.

He wasn't the cook, the butler, the gardener, or any of the hired hand. He was voted to be the President of this great land.

He stood against insurmountable odds, just because of the color of his skin. Even though he was more than qualified, there were those who thought he would never win.

During his campaign, racial hatred came at him like a shotgun. They hoped he would get discouraged, give in, claim defeat, and not continue to run.

44

PRESIDENT

RACISM
BULLYING
PREJUDICE
DISCRIMINATION
WHITE SUPREMACY

He was bullied by those whose titles would make you think that they were wise. But, by the grace of God, he won the race despite their evil lies.

They spread rumors like bullies do including about the place he was born. They even tried to disgrace his character with scandalous porn.

LIES, LIES AND MORE LIES!!!

In spite of their hatred, he served the Nation with dignity, for the first four years. All the while badgered by some with unfounded criticism, when they should've cheered.

He cleaned up the economic disaster left by another administration. He almost had to start revamping as far back as the earth's creation.

Beside him was who God said all men created in His image need. A woman with pure grace, intelligence and of the very best seed.

A seed that blooms so graciously, even in the storms of life. She's a gift from God, adorned with favor, to be a man's beautiful wife.

She's made virtuous, from the crown of her head, to the soles of her feet. She's the epitome of elegance, all so kind, polite, and sweet.

"What an honor to see her standing, within her own strengths," recalled the Butcher, "by the President's side. For the first time since Dr. Martin Luther King, Jr., the black nation was bursting with pride."

His presidential assigned number, 44, is the biblical number of chosen people from birth. It's rooted in the number 4, which is the number of the creation, particularly earth.

Putting it all together reveals that his appointment on earth was assured. It was ordained by God, as his destiny, therefore, secured.

The Butcher said proudly, "After four years, they stood together and strong to take on another presidential race. They won the election which kept the Nation's African American President four more years in his place."

"His place wasn't to him, by name, a white house dwelling that he maintained. The White House sacredly represented the nation's pain through all that they lost and gained."

"Each room is so elegantly designed with the finest décor. From the ornate ceiling, to the antique, java hardwood floor."

"It's all so grand, which makes it a historically, beautiful sight. Every piece of furniture, carpet, and curtain is kept tidy with windows polished bright."

But there is a deep dark stain that cannot be seen with the naked eye. It's the stain of prejudice behaviors, attitudes, and racist lies.

There were 11 presidents that were known for their racist acts. Belligerently making laws that they knew would degrade and keep down the blacks.

"How refreshing it was, interjected the Butcher, "that during this President's eight years, you never heard of anything racist coming out of the White House. If it happened, it wasn't socially publicized, it was kept as quiet as a daydreaming mouse."

"He said he was taught, 'Everything you think, doesn't have to come out of your mouth. It's loose lips that sink ships all the way to the Deep South.'"

"As their last term ended, the Nation prepared for a new commander and chief. The final lesson this President taught us was to keep his campaign slogan, 'Yes We Can,' as our belief."

"There were many sayings that kept them humble in their eight-year quest. By being selfless, they live a life, then and now, that is very blessed."

Unfortunately, the Nation installed a new commander and chief who the African American race never expected. Hidden behind his business attire was more than could have been detected.

He was elected as President by an antiquated system, not by majority vote. It didn't matter to him as he takes every opportunity to gloat.

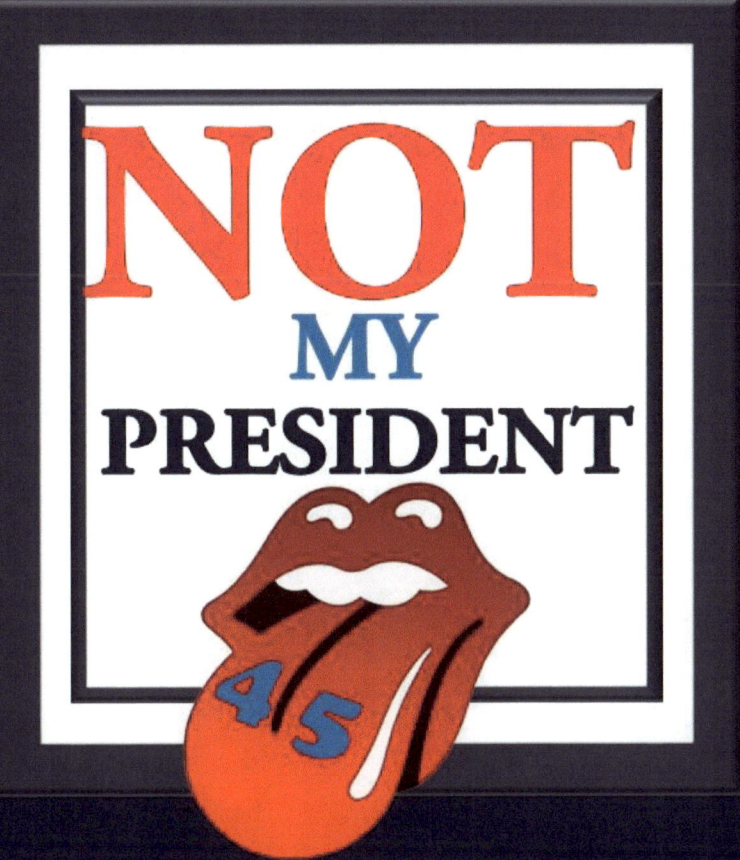

The black nation was so very disappointed, at this country's unbelievable choice. Most of the people refuse to speak his name; therefore, only his number comes from their voice.

He's not called the President or Commander in Chief, but number forty-five. The people even demanded a voter recount, to see if everyone listed as voted was actually alive.

We wouldn't be surprised to see a name like Elvis, on a hand-written ballot. It's a disgrace today we can't trust a president, police officer, or even a judge who holds a mallet.

The Butcher remarked, "This one truly can't be who the Nation thinks will make us 'Great Again.' There are cartoon characters that had better intentions like Chicken Little, Ducky Lucky, and Henny Penny, the hen."

Chickypooh was curious to hear about her cousin, Chicken Little, and her friends. Although she knew it was sad, the way that it ends.

So, she asked the Butcher to explain in details what he meant. She wanted him to be ever so specific about the entire event.

"Chicken Little, Ducky Lucky, and Henny Penny were running to tell the lion that the sky was falling. When they meet Foxey Loxey, who asked where they were going, as he was crawling."

"They said, 'the sky is falling, so we're going to tell the lion about it before it gives. Unfortunately, neither one of us knows where the courageous lion lives.'"

"Foxey Loxey's father said, 'I know where the lion's den, follow me as I lead the way.'"

" He led them into his cave instead, and that's the last anyone has seen of them since that very day."

Chickypooh sat there clutching her tablet, with tears falling from her eyes. She was emotional because it's hard for her to imagine that's how her cousin dies.

She was eaten by a fox who she trusted to be her guide. "All of us could be such a fool!" Chickypooh declared, as she cried.

Chickypooh said to the Butcher, "How could anyone be so cruel? He ended their life, and they were still in school."

Sadly, that's the character of who this Nation calls number forty-five. He pretends to have good intentions but his actions show he cares nothing about the people he leads lives.

He possesses the character of the biggest bully the world has ever seen. Low-down dirty, hateful, inconsiderate and mean.

Chickypooh, yet emotional, sobs, "Let's pause for today! I need to see the Baker now to hear what he has to say."

So, she snapped her fingers to awaken the Butcher from his trance. When the Butcher got up, he grabbed a fiddle and happily started to dance.

The Butcher asked, "What happened, I feel like a new man, my burdens lifted and free at last. Whatever you did, do it again so that I can get released from more of my past."

Chickypooh proclaimed, "There's a better way to keep free from ill feelings. Be extremely careful with whom you're dealing."

"Practice these two golden and important rules that are true. Love thy neighbor as thyself and do unto others only what you'd want to be done unto you."

"The amount of stress you will avoid you'll be amazed. Soon those things that troubled you before, you won't be a slight bit phased."

Chickypooh then called in the Baker
from making his daily bread. He brought in
with him a treat to make sure Chickypooh
was fed.

He said, "May I lay down on the sofa,"
before Chickypooh could even say hello.
"Please, let's get started. I can't wait to

"It doesn't matter to me," said the Baker all dressed in his clean black vest. "I saw the Butcher come out looking happy and a lot less stressed."

"See, my real name is Pinocchio; therefore, I'm living under a spell. My nose is extremely long because of the many lies I've chosen to tell."

"Mr. Geppetto made me and told me always to tell the truth. Each time that I didn't, my nose grew which at the time I was in my youth."

"I've been wanting to get from under this spell for quite some time. Just pull out your bell, blow a whistle or hit your magic chyme."

"I'm a willing participant in your quest for the answer, 'Why?'" So, the impatient Baker snapped his own fingers and let out a great big sigh.

Chickypooh began by asking the Baker "What do you do in the white house?" He responded, "I cook the very fine baked goods, along with my spouse."

"Tell me what you hear, coming from the Oval Room. Any heated conversations or objects were thrown as personalities fume?"

32

Here is what the Baker had to say:

It's apparent, everyone wasn't taught, "if you don't have anything good to say, don't say anything at all." Because this White House resident displays a new definition to catcall.

Catcall is a shrill whistle, shout of disapproval, typically one made in a public meeting. It's not, by any means, a pleasant salutation, sincere welcome or a polite greeting.

It's what bullies do as a chess move, to intimidate who they believe are weak. All their evil wrongdoings are done in your face, they aren't about to sneak.

He has turned social media into his sounding board, to alert the Nation of his next prejudice change. His offensive twitter attacks have hypothetically killed more people, than believed to have died from the hands of The Butcher of Plainfield, who was deranged.

"One day I said, 'Excuse me, Sir, could I speak with you about an urgent matter?' He screamed at me 'Go away you're a hired hand!' Then a glass he shattered."

"I only wanted to tell him that he had a big white piece of lent in the crouch of his pant. No one else dared to tell him because of their fear he would rant."

"Sure enough, they were right about his predicted animal-like behavior. They looked at me and said 'You better pray and call on your Savior.'"

"I hurried to exit his presence to retreat to the room I consider my haven. The way he stumped as he screamed, I thought the floor was about to cave in."

"From that day forward, it didn't matter what I saw on him that was out of place. It could've been dirty t-paper hanging from his waist, or rotten egg on his face."

"I just bow and nod with a grin that reflects what I see. All the staff laughs in hopes it stays in plain sight until he gets on TV."

"Often the three of us feel like the Three Little Pigs who were terrorized by the Big Bad Bear." "Wasn't it a wolf, asked Chickypooh, "with lots and lots of hair?"

"It may have been," replied the Baker, "but who cares they both hunt like a hound. They have long claws, very sharp teeth, and a horrifying sound."

"So, the wolf came, as he did to the little pigs, and said, 'Little pig, little pig, let me come in. No, no, no not by the hair on my chinny, chin chin. Then I'll huff, and I'll puff, and I'll blow your house in.'"

"The Big Bad Wolf blows down the first two pigs' houses, made of straw and sticks. But he's unable to destroy the third pig's house because, while she went swimming, she had her contractors build her house out of bricks."

Chickypooh thought to shed some light on one meaning of the fairy tale. "It's not about a physical house built with straws, bricks, or wood held together by nails."

"It's to teach us that our character should be built firm to withstand the storms that life brings. Lie's, false accusations, disappointments, heartaches and a list of the worst of things."

"If we don't, we'll crumble under pressure, just as soon as an unpleasant situation appears. Our character is strengthened, like a brick, each time we do what's right, no matter if it brings us to tears."

42

"I think it's time to end your session," says Chickypooh, "to bring in the Candlestick Maker. When I snap my fingers one, two, three, open your eyes, you'll then be The White House Baker."

"Hot diggity dog!" Screamed the Baker, as he leaped like the Pillsbury Doughboy to his feet. "I sense the desire to make a baker's dozen of apple pie which is America's most loved sweet."

"I can't wait to tell my wife, that from now on, how I will love to come to work. I feel now, being the Baker in The White House is such an awesome perk."

"I'm glad you've found new life," said Chickypooh, "by releasing your secret ills and woes. Now you can sincerely concentrate on your purpose which is making lots of dough."

"Just take a moment to tell the Candlestick Maker he's the last of the workers I'll see. And, to not to be sad to be the last to spend some time with me."

In came the Candlestick Maker with his head hung down, looking red-hot and somewhat sick. He barely made it to the sofa, because of the sparks coming from his wick.

Chickypooh said frantically, "That's not a candle it's a bomb ready to explode at the drop of a dime! It's not wise to hold on to things that can destroy you and others at any given time."

The Candlestick Maker looked at Chickypooh with only an ounce of flicker in his eyes. "Please, help me," he said in a weeping voice, "I beg of you before this flame dies."

"I'm not going to hypnotize you," replied Chickypooh, "for one simple and obvious reason. You possess the light; therefore, it's difficult for darkness to thrive in you at any time or season."

"Decree to whatever is keeping that bomb lit to cease and to let go. It doesn't have any power over you unless you declare it so.

"What you have to remember when confronted with darkness, is to turn up your light so that it glows. Darkness gives way not just to the light but to the spirit that it shows."

"So, I recommend that you place plenty of candles in each and every room. Upstairs, downstairs, in all the halls and living spaces, especially where it appears to be gloom."

"When the Big Bad Wolf comes to huff and puff to blow out your candle. Don't listen to the gossip, lies, insults, or scandals."

"Shield your light from that which you know to be false. Don't believe a word that's said, reject it, even if it comes from your boss."

All of a sudden, the Candlestick Maker lit up, as if he had won a million dollars. The knowledge Chickypooh gave him to change his life made him feel like a Rhodes Scholar.

If we could only teach number forty-five the same valuable lessons, Chickypooh has shared. His unfortunate fate of impeachment and humiliation may be spared.

We could put together both slogans "Yes We Can Be Great Again." It would be meant from the heart not just written with a pen.

All three workers were glad Chickypooh was able to help in ways they never expected. The Butcher, Baker and Candlestick Maker felt that the three of them were now so very connected.

"Based on the information that you've given me", said Chickypooh, "I realize none of what the Nation has heard is 'fake news.' It's founded on public perception, consistent personal interaction and up-close views."

"Just as important, I believe I've hit the answer to the Nation's question, 'Why?', Right between the bull's eye. With my mission being accomplished, I will say my final goodbye."

"We don't know the answer," said the Baker, "so can you share it with the three of us? Or, is it a national security secret; therefore, you cannot discuss?"

"No, it's not a secret," said Chickypooh. "I don't have anything to hide. The answer is, and has always been, 'to get to the other side!'"

About the Author

Evangelist Jacqueline Charmane is an extremely talented, gifted, anointed and formally ordained woman of God. In 1995, Jacqueline began performing nationally and internationally for theatrical productions. For nearly twenty-five years, Jacqueline has written, directed, and performed in stage plays, as well as designed spectacular fashions, costumes and dance wardrobes. In 1998, Jacqueline began performing gospel comedy that after a decade gave rise to the character "Mother Maeye." Jacqueline (as Mother Maeye) has been seen on *Black Entertainment Television's* (BET) website, over a dozen commercials for the famous gospel talent show *"Sunday Best"*, and has two live DVD recordings. As an author and playwright, Jacqueline has written and published 11 books, 3 plays.

SPECIAL ACKNOWLEDGEMENTS

Illustration Characters' Contributors:
Nicoleta Ifrim-Ionescu @123rf.com
Christos Georghiow @123rf.com
Blueringmedia@123rf.com
Teguh Mujiono @123rf.com
Sergey Vasiliev @123rf.com
Igor Zakowski@123rf.com
Monicabc@123rf.com
Abdul Rohim @123rf.com
Artisticcollc@123rf.com
Dedmezay@123rf,com
Dazdraperma @123rf.com
Hafakot @123rf.com
Putut Handoko @123rf.com
Rivusdea @123rf.com
iimages@123rf.com
3dimages@123rf.com
seamartini@123rd.com
Other Elements Contributors:
Clipart-library.com
Pnglibrary.com
Openclipart.org
Pngtree.com
Stickpng.com

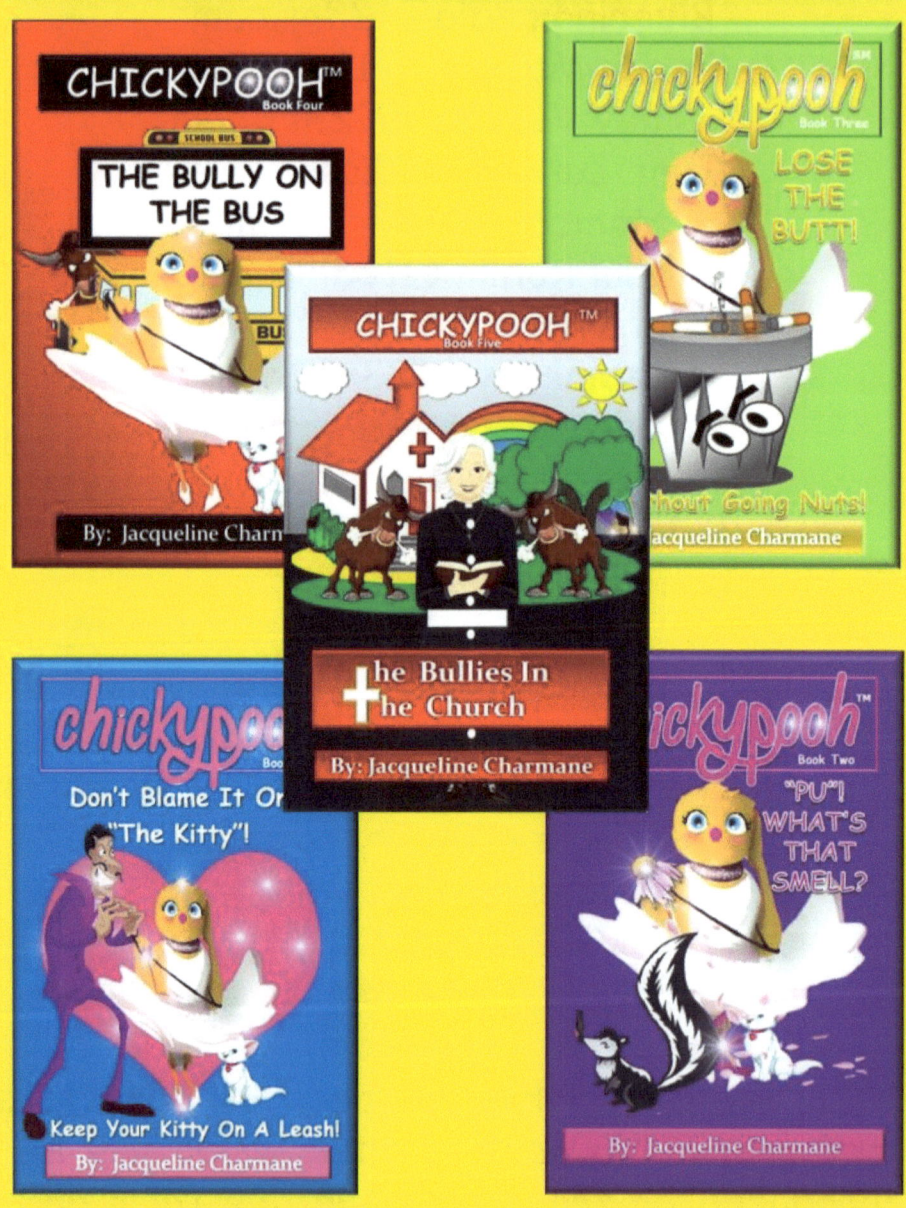

www.ingramcontent.com/pod-product-compliance
Lightning Source LLC
Chambersburg PA
CBHW041025170626
46815CB00001B/7